ADDRESS UNKNOWN

ALSO BY KATHRINE KRESSMANN TAYLOR

Day of No Return (Until That Day)
Diary of Florence in Flood (Ordeal by Water)
Jours d'orage (Storm on the Rock)
Ainsi rêvent les femmes
Ainsi mentent les hommes
Monsieur Pan

ADDRESS UNKNOWN

A NOVEL

KATHRINE KRESSMANN TAYLOR

ecco
An Imprint of HarperCollins*Publishers*

ADDRESS UNKNOWN. Copyright © 1938 by Kressmann Taylor. Copyright renewed © 1966, 2015 by C. Douglas Taylor. Afterword copyright © 2015 by C. Douglas Taylor. Introduction copyright © 2021 by Margot Livesey. All rights reserved. Printed in the United States of America. No part of this book may be used or reproduced in any manner whatsoever without written permission except in the case of brief quotations embodied in critical articles and reviews. For information, address HarperCollins Publishers, 195 Broadway, New York, NY 10007.

HarperCollins books may be purchased for educational, business, or sales promotional use. For information, please email the Special Markets Department at SPsales@harpercollins.com.

Ecco® and HarperCollins® are trademarks of HarperCollins Publishers.

Originally published in the United States in 1938 by Simon & Schuster Inc.

Published in the United Kingdom in 2019 by Serpent's Tail, an imprint of Profile Books Ltd.

Designed by Angela Boutin
Image on page 67 by James Alexander, Jade Design

Library of Congress Cataloging-in-Publication Data has been applied for.

ISBN 978-0-06-306849-0

21 22 23 24 25 LSC 10 9 8 7 6 5 4 3 2 1

INTRODUCTION

When I was growing up in Scotland, World War II still cast a long shadow. Sugar rationing did not end until 1953, meat rationing until 1954. The comic I read every week carried a story about Biggles, the intrepid pilot, flying lone missions, while Remembrance Day, when we had two minutes of silence at school and everyone wore poppies, was a deeply solemn occasion. After hearing about the prisoners of Colditz, I tried with two friends to dig an escape tunnel in the woods. I no longer remember what we were escaping from – only that we gave up after a few feet. Did we know about anti-Semitism? Very vaguely. My adoptive mother, who grew up in London during the 1930s, told me that everyone knew about the anti-Semitism in Germany – after Kristallnacht the Kindertransport brought nearly 10,000 Jewish children to London – but she didn't learn about the concentration camps until after the war ended. Her impression was that the adults around her knew nothing about them either.

Despite many subsequent wars, World War II still has a strong hold on our collective memories and imaginations; it is not only a part of history but also a part of our communal mythology, as the many books, fiction and nonfiction, published every year testify. Novelists can count on readers to know, in some detail, the main facts of the war and can shine a light on some new aspect of the struggle, as happens in Mamta Chaudhry's *Haunting Paris*, Kazuo Ishiguro's *The Remains of the Day*, Walter Kempowski's *All for Nothing*, Ian McEwan's *Atonement* and Jim Shepard's *The Book of Aron*, to name a few. These novelists are looking back, fully aware of the dramatic ironies. But Kathrine Kressmann Taylor's *Address Unknown* is not a historical novel. She was born in 1903 in Portland, Oregon, and she was writing about the present, about what she observed and understood in the world around her. The rapturous reception the novel received when it was published in 1938, under the name Kressmann Taylor, suggests that she was not alone in her awareness of what was happening in Europe, but few, if any, American novelists were writing about Hitler's rise to power. I read *Address Unknown* in November 2020, and I have been thinking about it ever since.

There are certain novels that have the remarkable quality of being both timely and prophetic. Think of Kafka's *The Trial*, Orwell's *1984*, Ellison's *Invisible Man* and Atwood's *The Handmaid's Tale*. Each creates a very particular world that simultaneously holds up a mirror to the present and suggests possibilities for the future. *Address Unknown* has this Janus-like quality. The novel consists entirely of letters (and one cablegram) written between two German friends, Max Eisenstein and Martin Schulse, who own a successful art gallery in San Francisco. Their correspondence begins in the autumn of 1932, when Martin moves back to Munich, and ends in the spring of 1934. What makes the novel still feel so timely are the confounding questions at the heart of the narrative: How do we know what we know, and when do we know it? Why does a good person become a bad person? What power does a citizen have against the state?

These questions felt urgent to Kressmann Taylor

eighty-three years ago, and they feel urgent now. In 2015, in Iowa City, I taught Ellison's *Invisible Man*, which was published in 1952. I remember beginning the class by writing on the board statistics for Black and white Americans: the mortality rates, the incarceration rates, the levels of education and income. The inequities Ellison had addressed were still, sadly, very much with us. After class I went out to dinner with my students, Black, Asian, Hispanic and white, all of us sitting around the table. Despite what I'd written on the board, I found myself thinking how fortunate we were to live in a time and place where we could work and talk as equals. Only later did I learn that afterward, walking home, my Black students carefully crossed the road to avoid the crowds of white people spilling out of the bars. As it did for many others, it took eight minutes and forty-six seconds on May 25, 2020, to make me realize how painfully limited my understanding was of the lives of Black Americans. The evidence was all around me, yet I had managed to have no idea of the ways in which racism, fear, authorized brutality and prejudice affected, to varying degrees, everyone in the Black community. When I went to investigate my mother's claim that the adults around her were ignorant of the camps,

I discovered that on June 25, 1942, the *Daily Telegraph* in London published a story with the headline 'Germans murder 700,000 Jews in Poland: Travelling Gas Chambers'. The article lists the numbers killed in various towns and cities, and describes the murder of children, pensioners and hospital patients. It was published on page five of a six-page issue of the paper and disappeared without a trace. No other newspapers took up the story.

Key to the success of the prophetic novel is that it is not a sermon. The reader wants to be informed but she longs to be entertained. Kressmann Taylor fulfills this longing by her gripping, fast-moving plot and her brilliant choice of the epistolary form. She may have come to the latter, as we learn in the afterword, almost accidentally, but she could scarcely have chosen a better way to explore her moral questions. The novel in letters has a long and lustrous history. There were already a number of notable examples when Aphra Behn, the first Englishwoman to earn her living by writing, published *Love-Letters Between a Nobleman and His Sister* in 1682, and many more were to follow. One of the signal advantages of the form is that it banishes the narrator's voice and moral stance; the letters represent only the point of view of the characters.

It also allows for a useful compression. Readers have a sense of eavesdropping; they don't expect to understand everything, or to learn every detail. Their assumption is that the letter writer has something important to communicate, and too much explaining can make a letter seem contrived. Kressmann Taylor makes excellent use of these attributes, particularly in the deft introduction of her third main character, Max's sister, Griselle, an actress who still lives in Europe and who, after years of struggle, is having great success on the stage in Vienna.

The voices of the two friends are pleasingly distinct – Max in San Francisco a little more colloquial, Martin in Munich a little more formal – but at the beginning of the novel they seem united in their attitudes. Max describes himself as selling the paintings Martin is sending over from Germany 'at an appalling profit' and delights in getting an indecent price for an ugly Madonna from old Mrs Fleshman. 'You speak of the poverty there', he writes. 'Conditions have been bad here this winter, but of course we have known nothing of the privations you see in Germany.' From the thirty-room house he's been able to buy so cheaply, Martin responds, 'The old despair has been thrown aside like a forgotten coat. No longer do the people wrap themselves in shame; they hope again.' The bad Jew-baiting, he writes, is only 'the little surface scum when a big movement boils up.' For many of Kressmann Taylor's contemporary readers, these words would have held no irony.

A few years after *Address Unknown* appeared, she went on to write a second novel, *Day of No Return*. It was based on interviews with a theological student who had been forced to flee Germany because he opposed Hitler's takeover of the Lutheran Church. In her introduction, Kressmann Taylor describes Hitler's plan to have the powerful church become a tool to disseminate Nazi doctrine. The Nazis succeed in taking over the church, 'but gradually,' she writes, 'they became aware that something was wrong. . . . A force was resisting them, something they could not put their hands on – a belief.' The novel was published shortly before Pearl Harbor brought America into the war.

While *Address Unknown* has remained timely over more than eighty years, there is one respect in which the world has definitively changed since its first publication. The novel is now being published under the author's full name, unmistakably identifying her as a woman. Whether this would have mattered to Kathrine Kressmann Taylor, I cannot say, but it matters to many of us who read her now.

Good novels, as the name promises, keep bringing us the news, and we read them with both our outer and our inner eyes. We bring to them the swirling chaos of the world around us and the seemingly endless negotiations between the forces of good and evil, and we bring to them our deep-seated, long-lasting preoccupations. *Address Unknown* satisfies both kinds of reading and offers the additional delights of a piercingly good story.

Margot Livesey

ADDRESS UNKNOWN

SCHULSE-EISENSTEIN GALLERIES

SAN FRANCISCO, CALIFORNIA, U.S.A.

NOVEMBER 12, 1932

Herrn Martin Schulse
Schloss Rantzenburg
Munich, Germany

My Dear Martin,

Back in Germany! How I envy you! Although
I have not seen it since my school days, the spell
of *Unter den Linden* is still strong upon me – the
breadth of intellectual freedom, the discussions,
the music, the light-hearted comradeship. And
now the old Junker spirit, the Prussian arrogance
and militarism are gone. You go to a democratic

Germany, a land with a deep culture and the beginnings of a fine political freedom. It will be a good life. Your new address is impressive and I rejoice that the crossing was so pleasant for Elsa and the young sprouts.

As for me, I am not so happy. Sunday morning finds me a lonely bachelor without aim. My Sunday home is now transported over the wide seas. The big old house on the hill – your welcome that said the day was not complete until we were together again! And our dear jolly Elsa, coming out beaming, grasping my hand and shouting 'Max, Max!' and hurrying indoors to open my favorite *Schnapps*. The fine boys, too, especially your handsome young Heinrich; he will be a grown man before I set eyes upon him again.

And dinner – shall I evermore hope to eat as I have eaten? Now I go to a restaurant and over my lonely roast beef come visions of *gebackener Schinken* steaming in its Burgundy sauce, of *Spaetzle*, ah! of *Spaetzle* and *Spargel*! No, I shall never again become reconciled to my American diet. And the wines, so carefully slipped ashore from the German boats, and the pledges we made as the glasses brimmed for the fourth and fifth and sixth times.

Of course you are right to go. You have never become American despite your success here, and now that the business is so well established you must take your sturdy German boys back to the homeland to be educated. Elsa too has missed her family through the long years and they will be glad to see you as well. The impecunious young artist has now become the family benefactor, and that too will give you a quiet little triumph.

The business continues to go well. Mrs Levine has bought the small Picasso at our price, for which I congratulate myself, and I have old Mrs Fleshman playing with the notion of the hideous Madonna. No one ever bothers to tell her that any particular piece of hers is bad, because they are all so bad. However I lack your fine touch in selling to the old Jewish matrons. I can persuade them of the excellence of the investment, but you alone had the fine spiritual approach to a piece of art that unarmed them. Besides they probably never entirely trust another Jew.

A delightful letter came yesterday from Griselle. She writes that she is about to make me proud of my little sister. She has the lead in a new play in Vienna and the notices are excellent – her discouraging years with the small companies are beginning to bear fruit. Poor child, it has not been easy for her, but she has never complained. She has a fine spirit, as well as beauty, and I hope the talent as well. She asked about you, Martin, in a very friendly way. There is no bitterness left there, for that passes quickly when one is young as she is. A few years and there is only a memory of the hurt, and of course neither of you was to be blamed. Those things are like quick storms, for a moment you are drenched and blasted, and you are so wholly helpless before them. But then the sun comes, and although you have neither quite forgotten, there remains only gentleness and no sorrow. You would not have had it otherwise, nor would I. I have not written Griselle that you are in Europe but perhaps I shall if you think it wise, for she does not make friends easily and I know she would be glad to feel that friends are not far away.

Fourteen years since the war! Did you mark the date? What a long way we have traveled, as peoples, from that bitterness! Again, my dear Martin, let me embrace you in spirit, and with the most affectionate remembrances to Elsa and the boys, believe me,

Your ever most faithful,
Max

SCHLOSS
RANTZENBURG

MUNICH, GERMANY

DECEMBER 10, 1932

Mr Max Eisenstein
Schulse-Eisenstein Galleries
San Francisco, California, U.S.A.

Max, Dear Old Fellow,

The check and accounts came through promptly, for which my thanks. You need not send me such details of the business. You know how I am in accord with your methods, and here at Munich I am in a rush of new activities. We are established, but what a turmoil! The house,

as you know, I had long in mind. And I got it at
an amazing bargain. Thirty rooms and about ten
acres of park; you would never believe it. But then,
you could not appreciate how poor is now this
sad land of mine. The servants' quarters, stables
and outbuildings are most extensive, and would
you believe it, we employ now ten servants for the
same wages of our two in the San Francisco home.

The tapestries and pieces we shipped make a
rich show and some other fine furnishings I have
been able to secure, so that we are much admired,
I was almost to say envied. Four full services in
the finest china I have bought and much crystal,
as well as a full service of silver for which Elsa is in
ecstasies.

And for Elsa – such a joke! You will, I know,
laugh with me. I have purchased for her a huge
bed. Such a size as never was before, twice the
bigness of a double bed, and with great posters
in carved wood. The sheets I must have made to

order, for there are no sheets made that could fit it. And they are of linen, the finest linen sheets. Elsa laughs and laughs, and her old *Grossmutter* stands shaking her head and grumbles, '*Nein*, Martin, *nein*. You have made it so and now you must take care or she will grow to match it.'

'*Ja*,' says Elsa, 'five more boys and I will fit it just nice and snug.' And she will, Max.

For the boys there are three ponies (little Karl and Wolfgang are not big enough to ride yet) and a tutor. Their German is very bad, being too much mixed with English.

Elsa's family do not find things so easy now. The brothers are in the professions and, while much respected, must live together in one house. To the family we seem American millionaires and while we are far from that yet our American income places us among the wealthy here. The better foods are high in price and there is much political unrest even now under the presidency of Hindenburg, a fine liberal whom I much admire.

Already old acquaintances urge me that I interest myself in administrative matters in the town. This I take under consideration. It may be somewhat to our benefit locally if I become an official.

As for you, my good Max, we have left you alone, but you must not become a misanthrope. Get yourself at once a nice fat little wife who will busy herself with all your cares and feed you into a good humor. That is my advice and it is good, although I smile as I write it.

You write of Griselle. So she wins her success, the lovely one! I rejoice with you, although even now I resent it that she must struggle to win her way, a girl alone. She was made, as any man can see, for luxury and for devotion and the charming and beautiful life where ease allows much play of the sensibilities. A gentle, brave soul is in her

dark eyes, but there is something strong as iron
and very daring too. She is a woman who does
nothing and gives nothing lightly. Alas, dear
Max, as always, I betray myself. But although you
were silent during our stormy affair, you know
that the decision was not easy for me. You never
reproached me, your friend, while the little sister
suffered, and I have always felt you knew that I
suffered too, most gravely. What could I do? There
was Elsa and my little sons. No other decision
was possible to make. Yet for Griselle I keep a
tenderness that will last long after she has taken a
much younger man for husband or lover. The old
wound has healed but the scar throbs at times, my
friend.

I wish that you will give her our address. We
are such a short distance from Vienna that she can
feel there is for her a home close at hand. Elsa, too,
knows nothing of the old feeling between us and
you know with what warmth she would welcome
your sister, as she would welcome you. Yes, you
must tell her that we are here and urge her to soon

make a contact with us. Give her our most warm congratulations for the fine success that she is making.

Elsa asks that I send to you her love, and Heinrich would also say 'hello' to Uncle Max. We do not forget you, Maxel.

My heartiest greetings to you,

Martin

SCHULSE-EISENSTEIN GALLERIES

SAN FRANCISCO, CALIFORNIA, U.S.A.

JANUARY 21, 1933

Herrn Martin Schulse
Schloss Rantzenburg
Munich, Germany

My Dear Martin,

I was glad to forward your address to Griselle. She should have it shortly, if she has not already received it. What jollification there will be when she sees you all! I shall be with you in spirit as heartily as if I also could rejoin you in person.

You speak of the poverty there. Conditions have been bad here this winter, but of course we have known nothing of the privations you see in Germany.

Personally, you and I are lucky that we have such a sound following for the gallery. Of course our own clientele are cutting their purchases but if they buy only half as much as before we shall be comfortable, not extravagantly so, but very comfortable. The oils you sent are excellent, and the prices are amazing. I shall dispose of them at an appalling profit almost at once. And the ugly Madonna is gone! Yes, to old Mrs Fleshman. How I gasped at her perspicacity in recognizing its worth, hesitating to set a price! She suspected me of having another client, and I named an indecent figure. She pounced on it, grinning slyly as she wrote her check. How I exulted as she bore the horror off with her, you alone will know.

Alas, Martin, I often am ashamed of myself for the delight I take in such meaningless little triumphs. You in Germany, with your country house and your affluence displayed before Elsa's relatives, and I in America, gloating because I have tricked a giddy old woman into buying a monstrosity. What a fine climax for two men of forty! Is it for this we spend our lives, to scheme for money and then to strut it publicly? I am always castigating myself, but I continue to do as before. Alas, we are all caught in the same mill. We are vain and we are dishonest because it is necessary to triumph over other vain and dishonest persons. If I do not sell Mrs Fleshman our horror, somebody else will sell her a worse one. We must accept these necessities.

But there is another realm where we can always find something true, the fireside of a friend, where we shed our little conceits and find warmth and understanding, where small selfishnesses are impossible and where wine and books and talk give a different meaning to existence. There we have made something that no falseness can touch. We are at home.

Who is this Adolf Hitler who seems rising toward power in Germany? I do not like what I read of him.

Embrace all the young fry and our abundant Elsa for

Your ever affectionate,
Max

SCHLOSS
RANTZENBURG

MUNICH, GERMANY

MARCH 25, 1933

Mr Max Eisenstein
Schulse-Eisenstein Galleries
San Francisco, California, U.S.A.

Dear Old Max,

You have heard of course of the new events
in Germany, and you will want to know how it
appears to us here on the inside. I tell you truly,
Max, I think in many ways Hitler is good for
Germany, but I am not sure. He is now the active
head of the government. I doubt much that even
Hindenburg could now remove him from power,

as he was truly forced to place him there. The
man is like an electric shock, strong as only a great
orator and a zealot can be. But I ask myself, is
he quite sane? His brown-shirt troops are of the
rabble. They pillage and have started a bad Jew-
baiting. But these may be minor things, the little
surface scum when a big movement boils up. For I
tell you, my friend, there is a surge – a surge. The
people everywhere have had a quickening. You
feel it in the streets and shops. The old despair has
been thrown aside like a forgotten coat. No longer
do the people wrap themselves in shame; they
hope again. Perhaps there may be found an end
to this poverty. Something, I do not know what,
will happen. A leader is found! Yet cautiously
to myself I ask, a leader to where? Despair
overthrown often turns us in mad directions.

Publicly, as is natural, I express no doubt. I
am now an official and a worker in the new regime
and I exult very loud indeed. All of us officials
who cherish whole skins are quick to join the
National Socialists. That is the name for Herr

Hitler's party. But also it is not only expedient, there is something more, a feeling that we of Germany have found our destiny and that the future sweeps toward us in an overwhelming wave. We too must move. We must go with it. Even now there are being wrongs done. The stormtroopers are having their moment of victory, and there are bloody heads and sad hearts to show for it. But these things pass; if the end in view is right they pass and are forgotten. History writes a clean new page.

All I now ask myself, and I can say to you what I cannot say to any here is: Is the end right? Do we make for a better goal? For you know, Max, I have seen these people of my race since I came here, and I have learned what agonies they have suffered, what years of less and less bread, of leaner bodies, of the end of hope. The quicksand of despair held them, it was at their chins. Then just before they died a man came and pulled them out. All they now know is, they will not die. They are in hysteria of deliverance, almost they worship him. But whoever the savior was, they would have done the same. God grant it is a true leader and no black angel they follow so joyously. To you alone, Max, I say I do not know. I do not know. Yet I hope.

So much for politics. Ourselves, we delight in our new home and have done much entertaining. Tonight the mayor is our guest, at a dinner for twenty-eight. We spread ourselves a little, maybe, but that is to be forgiven. Elsa has a new gown of blue velvet, and is in terror for fear it will not be big enough. She is with child again. There is the way to keep a wife contented, Max. Keep her so busy with babies she has no time to fret.

Our Heinrich has made a social conquest. He goes out on his pony and gets himself thrown off, and who picks him up but the Baron Von Freische. They have a long conversation about America, and one day the baron calls and we have coffee. Heinrich will go there to lunch next week.

What a boy! It is too bad his German is not better but he delights everyone.

So we go, my friend, perhaps to become part of great events, perhaps only to pursue our simple family way, but never abandoning that trueness of friendship of which you speak so movingly. Our hearts go out to you across the wide sea, and when the glasses are filled we toast 'Uncle Max'.

Yours in affectionate regard,
Martin

SCHULSE-EISENSTEIN GALLERIES

SAN FRANCISCO, CALIFORNIA, U.S.A.

MAY 18, 1933

Herrn Martin Schulse
Schloss Rantzenburg
Munich, Germany

Dear Martin,

I am in distress at the press reports that come pouring in to us from the Fatherland. Thus it is natural that I turn to you for light while there are only conflicting stories to be had here. I am sure things cannot be as bad as they are pictured. A terrible pogrom, that is the consensus of our American papers.

I know your liberal mind and warm heart
will tolerate no viciousness and that from you
I can have the truth. Aaron Silberman's son
has just returned from Berlin and had, I hear, a
narrow escape. The tales he tells of what he has
seen, floggings, the forcing of quarts of castor oil
through clenched teeth and the consequent hours
of dying through the slow agony of bursting guts,
are not pretty ones. These things may be true,
and they may, as you have said, be but the brutal
surface froth of human revolution. Alas, to us Jews
they are a sad story familiar through centuries of
repetition, and it is almost unbelievable that the
old martyrdom must be endured in a civilized
nation today. Write me, my friend, and set my
mind at ease.

Griselle's play will come to a close about
the end of June after a great success. She writes
that she has an offer for another role in Vienna
and also for a very fine one in Berlin for the
autumn. She is talking most of the latter one, but
I have written her to wait until the anti-Jewish

feeling has abated. Of course she uses another name which is not Jewish (Eisenstein would be impossible for the stage anyway), but it is not her name that would betray her origin. Her features, her gestures, her emotional voice proclaim her a Jewess no matter what she calls herself, and if this feeling has any real strength she had best not venture into Germany just at present.

Forgive me, my friend, for so distrait and brief a letter but I cannot rest until you have reassured me. You will, I know, write in all fairness. Pray do so at once.

With the warmest protestations of faith and friendship for you and yours, I am ever your faithful

Max

DEUTSCH-BÖLKISCHE BANK
UND HANDELSGESELLSCHAFT,

MÜNCHEN

JULY 9, 1933

Mr Max Eisenstein
Schulse-Eisenstein Galleries
San Francisco, California, U.S.A.

Dear Max,

You will see that I write upon the stationery of my bank. This is necessary because I have a request to make of you and I wish to avoid the new censorship which is most strict. We must for the present discontinue writing each other. It is impossible for me to be in correspondence with a Jew even if it were not that I have an official position to maintain. If a communication becomes necessary you must enclose it with the bank draft and not write to me at my house again.

As for the stern measures that so distress you, I myself did not like them at first, but I have come to see their painful necessity. The Jewish race is a sore spot to any nation that harbors it. I have never hated the individual Jew – yourself I have always cherished as a friend, but you will know that I speak in all honesty when I say I have loved you, not because of your race but in spite of it.

The Jew is the universal scapegoat. This does not happen without reason, and it is not the old superstition about 'Christ-killers' that makes them distrusted. But this Jew trouble is only an incident. Something bigger is happening.

If I could show you, if I could make you see – the rebirth of this new Germany under our Gentle

Leader! Not for always can the world grind a great people down in subjugation. In defeat for fourteen years we bowed our heads. We ate the bitter bread of shame and drank the thin gruel of poverty. But now we are free men. We rise in our might and hold our heads up before the nations. We purge our bloodstream of its baser elements. We go singing through our valleys with strong muscles tingling for a new work – and from the mountains ring the voices of Wodan and Thor, the old, strong gods of the German race.

But no. I am sure as I write, as with the new vision my own enthusiasm burns, that you will not see how necessary is all this for Germany. You will see only that your own people are troubled. You will not see that a few must suffer for the millions to be saved. You will be a Jew first and wail for your people. This I understand. It is the Semitic character. You lament but you are never brave enough to fight back. That is why there are pogroms.

Alas, Max, this will pain you, I know, but you must realize the truth. There are movements far bigger than the men who make them up. As for me, I am a part of the movement. Heinrich is an officer in the boys' corps which is headed by Baron Von Freische whose rank is now shedding a luster upon our house, for he comes often to visit with Heinrich and Elsa, whom he much admires. Myself, I am up to the ears in work. Elsa concerns herself little with politics except to adore our Gentle Leader. She gets tired too easily this last month. Perhaps the babies come too fast. It will be better for her when this one is born.

I regret our correspondence must close this way, Max. Perhaps we can someday meet again on a field of better understanding.

As ever your,
Martin Schulse

SCHULSE-EISENSTEIN GALLERIES

SAN FRANCISCO, CALIFORNIA, U.S.A.

AUGUST I, 1933

Herrn Martin Schulse
(kindness of J. Lederer)
Schloss Rantzenburg
Munich, Germany

Martin, My Old Friend,

I am sending this by the hand of Jimmy
Lederer, who will shortly pass through Munich
on a European vacation. I cannot rest after the
letter you last sent me. It is so unlike you I can
only attribute its contents to your fear of the
censorship. The man I have loved as a brother,

whose heart has ever been brimming with sympathy and friendship, cannot possibly partake of even a passive partnership in the butchery of innocent people. I trust and pray that it may be so, that you will write me no exposition, which might be dangerous for you – only a simple 'yes'. That will tell me that you play the part of expediency but that your heart has not changed, and that I was not deluded in believing you to be always a man of fine and liberal spirit to whom wrongs are wrongs in whosoever's name they may be committed.

This censorship, this persecution of all men of liberal thought, the burning of libraries and corruption of the universities would arouse your antagonism if there had been no finger laid on one of my race in Germany. You are a liberal, Martin. You have always taken the long view. I know that you cannot be swept away from sanity by a popular movement which has so much that is bad about it, no matter how strong it may be.

———

I can see why the Germans acclaim Hitler. They react against the very real wrongs which have been laid on them since the disaster of the war. But you, Martin, have been almost an American since the war. I know that it is not my friend who has written to me, that it will prove to have been only the voice of caution and expediency.

Eagerly I await the one word that will set my heart at peace. Write your 'yes' quickly.

My love to you all,
Max

AUGUST 18, 1933

Mr Max Eisenstein
Schulse-Eisenstein Galleries
San Francisco, California, U.S.A.

Dear Max,

I have your letter. The word is 'no'. You are a
sentimentalist. You do not know that all men are
not cut to your pattern. You put nice little tags
on them, like 'liberal' and expect them to act so-
and-so. But you are wrong. So, I am an American
liberal? No! I am a German patriot.

A liberal is a man who does not believe in doing anything. He is a talker about the rights of man, but just a talker. He likes to make a big noise about freedom of speech, and what is freedom of speech? Just the chance to sit firmly on the backside and say that whatever is being done by the active men is wrong. What is so futile as the liberal? I know him well because I have been one. He condemns the passive government because it makes no change. But let a powerful man arise, let an active man start to make a change, then where is your liberal? He is against it. To the liberal any change is the wrong one.

He calls this the 'long view', but it is merely a bad scare that he will have to do something himself. He loves words and high-sounding precepts but he is useless to the men who make the world what it is. These are the only important men, the doers. And here in Germany a doer has risen. A vital man is changing things. The whole tide of a people's life changes in a minute because the man of action has come. And I join him. I am not just swept along by a current. The useless life that was all talk and no accomplishment I drop. I put my back and shoulders behind the great new movement. I am a man because I act. Before that I am just a voice. I do not question the ends of our action. It is not necessary. I know it is good because it is so vital. Men are not drawn into bad things with so much joy and eagerness.

You say we persecute men of liberal thought, we destroy libraries. You should wake from your musty sentimentalizing. Does the surgeon spare the cancer because he must cut to remove it? We are cruel. Of course we are cruel. As all birth is brutal, so is this new birth of ours. But we rejoice. Germany lifts high her head among the nations of the world. She follows her Glorious Leader to triumph. What can you know of this, you who only sit and dream? You have never known a Hitler. He is a drawn sword. He is a white light, but hot as the sun of a new day.

I must insist that you write no further. We are no longer in sympathy, as now we must both realize.

Martin Schulse

EISENSTEIN GALLERIES

SAN FRANCISCO, CALIFORNIA, U.S.A.

SEPTEMBER 5, 1933

Herrn Martin Schulse
c/o Deutsch-Voelkische Bank
und Handelsgesellschaft
Munich, Germany

Dear Martin,

Enclosed are your draft and the month's
accounts. It is of necessity that I send a brief
message. Griselle has gone to Berlin. She is too
daring. But she has waited so long for success she
will not relinquish it, and laughs at my fears. She
will be at the Koenig Theater. You are an official.

For old friendship's sake, I beg of you to watch over her. Go to Berlin if you can and see whether she is in danger.

It will distress you to observe that I have been obliged to remove your name from the firm's name. You know who our principal clients are, and they will touch nothing now from a firm with a German name.

Your new attitude I cannot discuss. But you must understand me. I did not expect you would take up arms for my people because they are my people, but because you were a man who loved justice.

I commend my rash Griselle to you. The child does not realize what a risk she is taking. I shall not write again.

Goodbye, my friend,
Max

SAN FRANCISCO, CALIFORNIA, U.S.A.

Herrn Martin Schulse
c/o Deutsch-Voelkische Bank
und Handelsgesellschaft
Munich, Germany

Martin,

I write again because I must. A black
foreboding has taken possession of me. I wrote
Griselle as soon as I knew she was in Berlin
and she answered briefly. Rehearsals were going
brilliantly; the play would open shortly. My
second letter was more encouragement than

warning, and it has been returned to me, the
envelope unopened, marked only addressee
unknown, (*Adressat Unbekannt*). What a darkness
those words carry! How can she be unknown? It is
surely a message that she has come to harm. They
know what has happened to her, those stamped
letters say, but I am not to know. She has gone
into some sort of void and it will be useless to seek
her. All this they tell me in two words, *Adressat
Unbekannt*.

Martin, need I ask you to find her to succor
her? You have known her graciousness, her beauty
and sweetness. You have had her love, which she
has given to no other man. Do not attempt to
write to me. I know I need not even ask you to aid.
It is enough to tell you that something has gone
wrong, that she must be in danger.

I leave her in your hands, for I am helpless.

Max

EISENSTEIN GALLERIES

SAN FRANCISCO, CALIFORNIA, U.S.A.

Herrn Martin Schulse
c/o Deutsch-Voelkische Bank
und Handelsgesellschaft
Munich, Germany

Martin,

I turn to you in despair. I could not wait for
another month to pass so I am sending some
information as to your investments. You may wish
to make some changes and I can thus enclose my
appeal with a bank letter.

It is Griselle. For two months there has been only silence from her, and now the rumors begin to come in to me. From Jewish mouth to Jewish mouth the tales slowly come back from Germany, tales so full of dread I would close my ears if I dared, but I cannot. I must be sure.

She appeared in the Berlin play for a week. Then she was jeered from the audience as a Jewess. She is so headstrong, so foolhardy, the splendid child! She threw the word back in their teeth. She told them proudly that she *was* a Jewess.

Some of the audience started after her. She ran backstage. Someone must have helped her for she got away with the whole pack at her heels and took refuge with a Jewish family in a cellar for several days. After that she changed her appearance as much as she could and started south, hoping to walk back to Vienna. She did not dare try the railroads. She told those she left that she would be safe if she could reach friends in Munich. That is my hope, that she has gone to you, for she has never reached Vienna. Send me word, Martin, and if she has not come there make a quiet investigation if you can. My mind cannot rest. I torture myself by day and by night, seeing the brave little thing trudging all those long miles through hostile country, with winter coming on. God grant you can send me a word of relief.

Max

Deutsch-Bölkische Bank und Handelsgesellschaft,

München

DECEMBER 8, 1933

Heil Hitler! I much regret that I have bad news for you. Your sister is dead. Unfortunately she was, as you have said, very much a fool. Not quite a week ago she came here, with a bunch of stormtroopers right behind her. The house was very active – Elsa has not been well since little Adolf was born last month – the doctor was here, and two nurses, with all the servants and children scurrying around.

By luck I answer the door. At first I think it is an old woman and then I see the face, and then I see the stormtroopers have turned in the park gates. Can I hide her? It is one chance in

47

thousands. A servant will be on us at any minute. Can I endure to have my house ransacked with Elsa ill in bed and to risk being arrested for harboring a Jew and to lose all I have built up here? Of course as a German I have one plain duty. She has displayed her Jewish body on the stage before pure young German men. I should hold her and turn her over to the stormtroopers. But this I cannot do.

'You will destroy us all, Griselle,' I tell her. 'You must run back further in the park.' She looks at me and smiles (she was always a brave girl) and makes her own choice.

'I would not bring you harm, Martin,' she says, and she runs down the steps and out toward the trees. But she must be tired. She does not run very fast and the stormtroopers have caught sight of her. I am helpless. I go in the house and in a few minutes she stops screaming, and in the morning I have the body sent down to the village for burial. She was a fool to come to Germany. Poor little

Griselle. I grieve with you, but as you see, I was helpless to aid her.

I must now demand you do not write again. Every word that comes to the house is now censored, and I cannot tell how soon they may start to open the mail to the bank. And I will no longer have any dealings with Jews, except for the receipt of money. It is not so good for me that a Jewess came here for refuge, and no further association can be tolerated.

A new Germany is being shaped here. We will soon show the world great things under our Glorious Leader.

Martin

CABLEGRAM

MUNICH JANUARY 2 1934

MARTIN SCHULSE

YOUR TERMS ACCEPTED NOVEMBER TWELVE
AUDIT SHOWS THIRTEEN PERCENT INCREASE
FEBRUARY SECOND FOUR-FOLD ASSURED PAN
EXHIBITION MAY FIRST PREPARE LEAVE FOR
MOSCOW IF MARKET OPENS UNEXPECTEDLY
FINANCIAL INSTRUCTIONS MAILED NEW
ADDRESS

EISENSTEIN

EISENSTEIN GALLERIES

SAN FRANCISCO, CALIFORNIA, U.S.A.

JANUARY 3, 1934

Herrn Martin Schulse
Schloss Rantzenburg
Munich, Germany

Our Dear Martin,

   Don't forget grandma's birthday. She will be
64 on the 8th. American contributors will furnish
1,000 brushes for your German Young Painters'
League. Mandelberg has joined in supporting the
league. You must send 11 Picasso reproductions,
20 by 90 to branch galleries on the 25th, no
sooner. Reds and blues must predominate. We can

allow you $8,000 on this transaction at present.
Start new accounts book 2.

Our prayers follow you daily, dear brother,

Eisenstein

EISENSTEIN GALLERIES
SAN FRANCISCO, CALIFORNIA, U.S.A.

JANUARY 17, 1934

Herrn Martin Schulse
Schloss Rantzenburg
Munich, Germany

Martin, Dear Brother,

Good news! Our stock reached 116 five days ago. The Fleishmans have advanced another $10,000. This will fill your Young Painters' League quota for a month but let us know if opportunities increase. Swiss miniatures are having a vogue. You must watch the market and plan to be in Zurich after May first if any unexpected opportunities develop. Uncle Solomon will be glad to see you and I know you will rely heavily on his judgment.

The weather is clear and there is little danger of storms during the next two months. You will prepare for your students the following reproductions: Van Gogh 15 by 103, red; Poussin 20 by 90, blue and yellow; Vermeer 11 by 33, red and blue.

Our hopes will follow your new efforts.

Eisenstein

EISENSTEIN GALLERIES

SAN FRANCISCO, CALIFORNIA, U.S.A.

JANUARY 29, 1934

Dear Martin,

Your last letter was delivered by mistake at 457 Geary St., Room 4. Aunt Rheba says tell Martin he must write more briefly and clearly so his friends can understand all that he says. I am sure everyone will be in readiness for your family reunion on the 15th. You will be tired after these festivities and may want to take your family with you on your trip to Zurich.

Before leaving however, procure the following reproductions for branches of German Young Painters' League, looking forward to the joint exhibit in May or earlier: Picasso 17 by 81, red; Van Gogh 5 by 42, white; Rubens 15 by 204, blue and yellow.

Our prayers are with you.

Eisenstein

SCHLOSS RANTZENBURG

MUNICH, GERMANY

FEBRUARY 12, 1934

Mr Max Eisenstein
Eisenstein Galleries
San Francisco, California, U.S.A.

Max, My Old Friend,

My God, Max, do you know what you do? I
shall have to try to smuggle this letter out with
an American I have met here. I write an appeal
from a despair you cannot imagine. This crazy
cable! These letters you have sent. I am called in
to account for them. The letters are not delivered,
but they bring me in and show me letters from you

and demand I give them the code. A code? And
how can you, a friend of long years, do this to me?

Do you realize, have you any idea that you
destroy me? Already the results of your madness
are terrible. I am bluntly told I must resign my
office. Heinrich is no longer in the boys' corps.
They tell him it will not be good for his health.
God in heaven, Max, do you see what that means?
And Elsa, to whom I dare not tell anything,
comes in bewildered that the officials refuse her
invitations and Baron Von Freische does not speak
to her upon the street.

Yes, yes, I know why you do it – but do you
not understand I could do nothing? What could I
have done? I did not dare to try. I beg of you, not
for myself, but for Elsa and the boys – think what
it means to them if I am taken away and they do
not know if I live or die. Do you know what it is
to be taken to a concentration camp? Would you
stand me against a wall and level the gun? I beg
of you, stop. Stop now, while everything is not

yet destroyed. I am in fear for my life, for my life, Max.

Is it you who does this? It cannot be you. I have loved you like a brother, my old Maxel. My God, have you no mercy? I beg you, Max, no more, no more! Stop while I can be saved. From a heart filled with old affection I ask it.

Martin

EISENSTEIN GALLERIES

SAN FRANCISCO, CALIFORNIA, U.S.A.

FEBRUARY 15, 1934

Herrn Martin Schulse
Schloss Rantzenburg
Munich, Germany

Our Dear Martin,

Seven inches of rainfall here in 18 days. What a season! A shipment of 1,500 brushes should reach the Berlin branch for your painters by this weekend. This will allow time for practice before the big exhibition. American patrons will help with all the artists' supplies that can be provided, but you must make the final arrangements. We

are too far out of touch with the European market
and you are in a position to gauge the extent of
support such a showing would arouse in Germany.
Prepare these for distribution by March 24th:
Rubens 12 by 77, blue; Giotto 1 by 317, green and
white; Poussin 20 by 90, red and white.

Young Blum left last Friday with the Picasso
specifications. He will leave oils in Hamburg
and Leipzig and will then place himself at your
disposal.

Success to you!

Eisenstein

EISENSTEIN GALLERIES

SAN FRANCISCO, CALIFORNIA, U.S.A.

MARCH 3, 1934

Martin Our Brother,

Cousin Julius has two nine-pound boys. The family is happy. We regard the success of your coming artists' exhibition as assured. The last shipment of canvases was delayed due to difficulties of international exchange but will reach your Berlin associates in plenty of time. Consider reproduction collection complete. Your best support should come from Picasso enthusiasts but neglect no other lines.

———◆———

We leave all final plans to your discretion but urge an early date for wholly successful exhibit.

The God of Moses be at your right hand.

Eisenstein

AFTERWORD

When *Address Unknown* was first published in the United States, in *Story* magazine in September 1938, it caused an immediate sensation. Written as a series of letters between a Jewish American living in San Francisco and his former business partner, returned to Germany, the story, early on, exposed the poison of Nazism to the American public.

Within ten days of publication, the entire printing of that issue of *Story* was sold out, and enthusiastic readers were mimeographing copies of the story to send to friends. National radio commentator Walter Winchell heartily recommended the story as 'the best piece of the month, something you shouldn't miss', and *Reader's Digest* put aside its long-standing no-fiction rule to reprint the piece for its more than three million readers.

In 1939, Simon & Schuster published *Address Unknown* as a book and sold 50,000 copies – a huge number in those years. Hamish Hamilton followed suit in England with a British edition, and foreign translations were begun. But 1939 was also the year of *Blitzkrieg*; within months most of Europe was under the domination of Adolf Hitler, the Dutch translation disappeared, and the only other European appearance of *Address Unknown* was on the *Reichskommissar*'s list of banned books. So the story remained unknown on the Continent for the next sixty years, despite its great impact and success in the US and England.

Author Kathrine Kressmann Taylor, 'the woman who jolted America', was born Kathrine Kressmann in Portland, Oregon, in 1903. After graduating from the University of Oregon in 1924, she moved to San Francisco and worked as an advertising copywriter, in her spare time writing for some small literary journals. In 1928 the editors of the *San Francisco Review*, a magazine she particularly liked, invited her to a party where she met Elliott Taylor, the owner of his own advertising agency, and they were married within two weeks. When the Great Depression put an end to the advertising industry, the couple bought a small farm in Southern Oregon, where they literally 'lived off the land', growing their own food and panning gold, taking their two small children and adding a third in 1935.

In 1938 they moved to New York, where Elliott worked as an editor, and Kathrine finished writing *Address Unknown*. Elliott showed it to *Story* magazine editor Whit Burnett, who immediately wished to publish it. He and Elliott decided that the story was 'too strong to appear under the name of a woman', and assigned Kathrine the literary pseudonym 'Kressmann Taylor', a professional name she accepted and kept for the rest of her life, largely because of the success of *Address Unknown*. This is how she describes the original motivation for the story:

A short time before the war, some cultivated, intellectual, warm-hearted German friends of mine returned to Germany after living in the United States. In a very short time they turned into sworn Nazis. They refused to listen to the slightest criticism about Hitler. During a return visit to California, they met an old dear friend of theirs on the street, who had been very close to them and who was a Jew. They did not speak to him. They turned their backs on him when he held his hands out to embrace them. *How can such a thing happen?* I wondered. *What changed their hearts so? What steps brought them to such cruelty?*

These questions haunted me very much and I could not forget them. It was hard to believe that these people whom I knew and respected had fallen victim to the Nazi poison. I began researching Hitler and reading his speeches and the writings of his advisors. What I discovered was terrifying. What worried me most was that no one in America was aware of what was happening in Germany and they also did not care. In 1938, the isolationist movement in America was strong; the politicians said that affairs in Europe were none of our business and that Germany was fine. Even Charles Lindbergh came back from Germany saying how wonderful the people were. But there were some students who returned from studying in Germany, and they told the truth about the Nazi atrocities. When their fraternity brothers had thought it would be fun to send them letters making fun of Hitler, they had written back and said, 'Stop it. We're in danger. These people don't fool around. You could murder one of these Nazis by writing letters to him.'

When that incident occurred, it made only a small article in the news, but it caught Elliott's eye; he brought it home to Kathrine, and it gave rise to their joint idea of using a letter as a weapon. She took that idea and went to work on the story she wanted to write.

I wanted to write about what the Nazis were doing and show the American public what happens to real, living people swept up in a warped ideology.

The result was *Address Unknown*, a great success about which the *New York Times Book Review* stated in 1939, 'This modern story is perfection itself. It is the most effective indictment of Nazism to appear in fiction.' That indictment continued in her next book, *Until That Day*, published in 1942, and reissued as *Day of No Return* in 2003.

Following the war, when any further indictment of the Nazis seemed no longer necessary, *Address Unknown* slipped from public notice and was largely forgotten, other than its inclusion in an occasional anthology. Elliott Taylor died in 1953, and Kathrine lived as a widow for the next fifteen years, continuing to write and to teach writing, journalism, and humanities at Gettysburg College, in Pennsylvania. Retiring in 1966, she moved to Florence, Italy, where she experienced the great flood of the Arno river in November of that year which inspired her third book, *Diary of Florence in Flood*, published to critical acclaim in both England and America the following spring.

En route to Italy in 1966 on the Italian Line's *Michelangelo*, Kathrine met the American sculptor John Rood. The two felt an immediate attraction, had a shipboard romance, and were married the following year in Minneapolis, where he made his home. Thereafter, they lived part of each year in Minneapolis, part in the Val di Pesa, outside Florence. Even after Rood's death in 1974, Kathrine kept both homes for nearly twenty years, living quietly in each six months a year, simply as Mrs John Rood.

Then, in 1995, when she was ninety-one years old, Story Press reissued *Address Unknown*, 'to commemorate the fiftieth anniversary of the liberation of the concentration camps,' and because, as *Story* editor Lois Rosenthal wrote, its 'significant and timeless message' had earned it 'a permanent place on the bookshelves' of America. The book was well-received, and Kathrine, happily signing copies and granting television and press interviews, was gratified at its re-emergence, this time with the stature of a classic of American literature.

Kathrine Kressmann Taylor Rood died the following year, in July 1996, late in her ninety-third year, sharp-witted, perceptive, and enthusiastic, even about the end of life. 'Dying,' she said in her last week, 'is normal. It's as normal as being born.' And she was ready. She had lived several successful lives: as a wife and mother, as a popular professor, and as the author of four books and a dozen short stories, one of which, *Address Unknown*, had been recognized as a classic while she lived.

Shortly after her death, a copy of the 1995 reissue came into the hands of French publisher Henry Dougier, of Éditions Autrement, Paris. He saw at once its relevance to the entire European community, both those who had lived under the Nazi domination and those who needed to know what it had been like. He determined that a French translation must be undertaken, and that translation, by Michèle Lévy-Bram, hit the French bestseller list in late 1999. *Inconnu à cette adresse* sold 50,000 copies that first year; 100,000 the next, and another 250,000 since, selling far more than it ever had in the United States. Soon other Europeans were reading it, calling for its translation and publication in their own languages: Spanish, Catalan, Gallego, Basque, Italian, Dutch, German, Norwegian, Swedish, Danish, Portuguese, Polish, Czech, and now from the rest of the world as well – Greek, Turkish, Korean, Chinese, Japanese and others (twenty-three languages by 2010).

The great success of *Address Unknown* in book form has led to other successes: audio books in German, Italian and French; radio productions in England, France, Israel and Croatia; live theater productions in France, Israel, Turkey, Italy, Belgium, Holland, Argentina, the US, including off-Broadway in 2004, and in both French and English at the Soho Theatre in London in 2013.

It is exciting to see this little book recognized as a classic, and it is gratifying that my mother lived to see its recognition as such with the 1995 Story Press edition, and to authorize in her last year the first of many translations –

into Hebrew, by the noted scholar/translator Asher Tarmon of Israel.

What the world will know of this story in future generations is hard to imagine, but it now seems that it will survive and will be included in the significant literature of the twentieth century.

Charles Douglas Taylor,
son of Kathrine Kressmann Taylor